# The Witch with an Itch

# Dragon v Dinosaur

## Helen Baugh

## Deborah Allwright

The littlest witch
and the wizard,
her twin,
were both very stubborn
and both liked to win.

So when a red envelope
plopped on the mat . . .

. . . in no time at all
it had started a spat.

"I want to
open it!"

"Give it
to me!"

The witch and the wizard
just could not agree.

They pulled and they tugged till the envelope tore
and the paper inside floated down to the floor:

Please come to my fancy-
dress party at three.
There's a prize for best costume
and cream cake for tea!

"**MY costume,**"
the witch said,
"**will beat all
the rest.**"

"**NO!**"
cried the wizard.
"**MINE will
be best.**"

The witch knew at once what she wanted to be
and she uttered a spell in a voice full of glee.

"Hobble and bobble and bobbity-bess.

Make me look just like a pretty princess!"

Her outfit was perfect – she wore a gold crown,
and rosy pink shoes and a pale lilac gown.

She whirled and she waltzed
round and round in her dress,
in no doubt her costume would bring her success.

The wizard's wand started to quiver and glow,
as he chanted HIS spell in a voice deep and low.

"Abracadabra and dabraca-down.

Make me look just like a colourful clown!"

His green hair was curly,
he had a red nose,
and long purple shoes
that curled up at the toes.

He threw pails of glitter
all over the place,

and squirted blue goo
in his poor sister's face.

The witch (dripping goo) was incensed at his cheek.
She pointed her wand and then started to speak.

"Hobble and bobble and flippity-flip. Make me the captain of a pirate ship!"

With eye-patch and parrot
and sharp silver hook,
the witch was delighted
with her pirate look.

She made a dramatic piratic marauder –
a captain of chaos and rampant disorder.

The wizard was speechless!
What could he do now?
He thought long and hard
with a deep-furrowed brow.

"Abracadabra
and dabra-delight.
Make me
a
dashing
and
valiant
knight!"

His helmet, his sword
and his armour were shiny,

he felt **big** and brave
(even though he was tiny).

The contest continued
for ten minutes longer.

First she was bigger . . .

then he was stronger.

Then she was furry . . .

then he was hairy.

Then she was spooky . . .

then he was scary.

This couldn't go on!
They had reached a stalemate.
Their battle would never
be done at this rate.

Then the witch
thought of something
– a genius spell!

The one that would
win her the fight
(she could tell).

"Hobble and bobble and dippity-door.

Make me a hungry and huge dinosaur!"

Quick as a flash she grew ten times her size,
with sharp pointy teeth
and green angry eyes.

The wizard (afraid that he might end up eaten) had one spell to try out before he was beaten.

"Abracadabra and dabraca-flagon. Make me a ginormous, fire-breathing dragon!"

Quick as a flash he grew
ten times HIS size,
with hot smoky breath
and red flashing eyes.

The two deadly beasts
were preparing to fight,
one willing to **burn**
and one ready to **bite**.

They seemed to forget
they were sister and brother,
each thinking only
of harming the other.

BUT . . .

. . . then the huge dinosaur started to twitch.
Her beastly behaviour had summoned the
ITCH!

(The witch got an itch when she did something wrong,
and with danger involved it was sure to be strong!)

The dinosaur started to **wriggle** and **ROAR**, then

(scritching and scratching)

**CRASHED** down to the floor.

Two precious wands took the force of the fall –
with THAT great big bottom,
they'd no chance at all!

The spells were both broken,
        thanks to the itch.

The battle was over for wizard and witch.

"But look at our wands!"
cried the twins in despair.
"Our magic has gone,
so now what will we wear?"

The party got started at three on the dot,
with loads of great fancy dress
costumes to spot.

A teapot, a starfish, a robot, a snake . . .
a giant who ate lots and lots of cream cake.
A spaceman, a flower, a mermaid, a lizard . . .
but nothing was seen of the witch
or the wizard.

So who won the prize for the best fancy dress?
The fairy? The monkey? No! You'll never guess!

The **wizard** and **witch**
won best costume of all,

for the **giant** . . .

who turned out to be two twins tall!

And when new wands arrived, they knew just what to do –

a treat was in store for their friends, old and new!

The twins used their magic to play, not to fight,
so their spells worked out well . . .

. . . with
no itches
in sight.

For my brother Ian,
love H.B.

For Madeleine,
love D.A.

DRAGON V DINOSAUR   A JONATHAN CAPE BOOK 978 0 857 55102 3
Published in Great Britain by Jonathan Cape, an imprint of Random House
Children's Publishers UK   A Penguin Random House Company

Penguin
Random House
UK

This edition published 2015   10 9 8 7 6 5 4 3 2 1

Text copyright © Helen Baugh, 2015
Illustrations copyright © Deborah Allwright, 2015
The right of Helen Baugh and Deborah Allwright to be identified as the author
and illustrator of this work has been asserted in accordance with the Copyright,
Designs and Patents Act 1988.

Random House Children's Publishers UK,
61-63 Uxbridge Road, London W5 5SA
www.randomhousechildrens.co.uk   www.randomhouse.co.uk
Addresses for companies within The Random House Group Limited can be found at:
www.randomhouse.co.uk/offices.htm
THE RANDOM HOUSE GROUP Limited Reg. No. 954009

A CIP catalogue record for this book is available from the British Library.
Printed in China

Penguin Random House is committed to a sustainable future for our business, our readers and our planet.
This book is made from Forest Stewardship Council® certified paper.

FSC
www.fsc.org
MIX
Paper from
responsible sources
FSC® C018179